Too Big and Heavy

written by Pam Holden
illustrated by Samer Hatam

1

On Monday, Baby Elephant went to
the playground with his friends.
He got on the seesaw, but he
couldn't go up and down.
Crack! The seesaw broke!

"Go away, Baby Elephant!
You can't play in our playground,"
shouted the animals.
"Go home! You're too big and heavy
to play here."

Baby Elephant went home. He felt sad.
"I'm too heavy to go on the seesaw,"
he told the big elephants.
"I wish I could go up and down like
my friends."

So the big elephants got a log
to make a seesaw for him.
Baby Elephant went up and down
on his own seesaw.
He felt very happy.

On Tuesday, Baby Elephant went
to the playground again.
He wanted to go on the swing,
but he got stuck!
"You're too big and heavy to go
on our swing!" said the animals.
So Baby Elephant went home.

The big elephants put out their
trunks to make a swing for him.
"Here's a good swing for you,"
they said.
Baby Elephant felt very happy
swinging on his own swing.

On Wednesday, Baby Elephant was hot.
He went into the swimming pool,
but all the water splashed out.
"Go home!" shouted the animals.
"You're too big for our pool."

The big elephants got water in their
trunks and they squirted him.
"Here's a fan to make you cool,"
they said, and they flapped their
big ears like a fan.
Baby Elephant felt cool and happy.

On Thursday, Baby Elephant felt
sad again.
"I can't play on the trampoline.
I'm too heavy to jump up and down
on it," he said.

10

So the big elephants put their trunks
together to make a trampoline for
Baby Elephant.
"Now you can jump and bounce,"
they said.

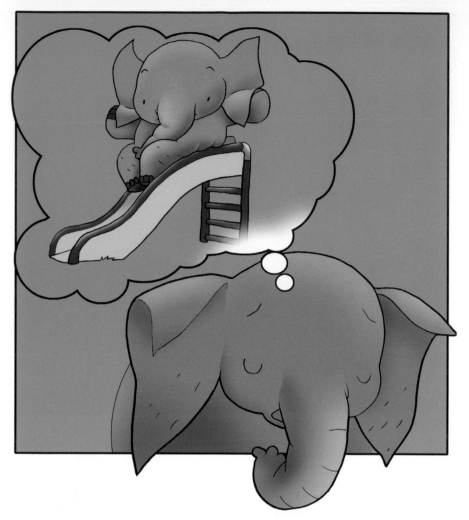

On Friday, Baby Elephant wanted
to have a slide.
"I wish I could play sliding with
my friends," he said.
"But I'm too big and heavy to go
on the slide."

So the big elephants put out their
trunks to make a slide for him.
"Wheee! This is a very good slide,"
he shouted.

On Saturday, the animals could hear someone laughing and splashing. "Who's that having fun?" they asked.

The animals saw Baby Elephant
playing with the big elephants.
They were swinging and sliding
and having fun.
They were laughing and happy.

On Sunday, the animals asked,
"Could we play with you in
your playground please?"
"Oh yes," said Baby Elephant.
"You're welcome every day!"

16